THE HUMANS AND I

EMIL KERT

Copyright © 2020 Emil Kert

All rights reserved. No part of this publication may be reproduced, stored, or transmitted in any form by any means, electronic, mechanical, photocopying, recording, scanning or otherwise, without written permission from the publisher. It is illegal to copy this book, post it to a website, or distribute it by another means without permission.

First Edition.

ISBN 978-0-646-82601-1

Cover design by Tanmaya Baluni

About the Author

I truly believe in stories. Stories that can not only change the viewpoint of a reader but can also change the world. People are so diverse, though. I think that everyone perceives information differently. There is a lot of compounded clutter out there nowadays; and so, through my passion for continuously exploring life and learning its ins and outs, I fell in love with explaining complex topics by weaving them into stories.

If you enjoy reading *The Humans and I* and you have other topics of interest which you would like me to weave into a story, then sign up here to tell me about it. Or, if you just want to be kept in the loop of upcoming new book releases, join my newsletter here.

I always love to hear from readers. If there is anything you'd like to share, or you just want to say *hi*, drop me a line at lime.kert@gmail.com.

Contents

To my partner in crime and companion in life, Sarah.

If I may borrow from a genius friend Isaac: What we know is a drop, what we don't know is an ocean.

One

Echolocation

It's so irritating! Soaring through the sky at night, it's like having a blindfold on. I can't see a single damn thing. Oh, I hate when they get so active at night. So much noise. If only someone could make those bats stop or teach them how to fly a little bit more gracefully. Ugh, all this squeaking all night. Even duplicating gets hard when the centrifugal forces are whipping me left, right, and center. I swear to God, if this doesn't stop soon, I'll rethink the viability of this bat host and start drafting an exit plan. Though on other hand, that seems like a waste. Since we are already in. How do I like to say? A new night, a new worksite.

Oh God, we finally came to a halt. Upside down, mind you, but better than being flung around.

"Ok, everyone: to all the virions, rookies, recruits, and established troops, get into position. I need all available viral rookies to locate new cells to invade. You recruits over there, head over to the lymphatic system and spread out. You should know by now where everything is in this bat, so no strolling or slacking. Chop, chop!"

"But sir, what about the imm—"

Ah, there he is. The only other cell that can actually respond and talk to me, my little assistant, Control. He's helping me out regulating our viral activity throughout our hosts. I think everyone should have their own Control. It's not only handy but it also frees you up to, you know, do whatever else you want to do. He's basically like a molecular-sized viral intern that you can pass on all the annoying and boring things to that you can't bother to do. He's a little bit of a slow learner and a bit of a greenhorn, actually, but all in all, he's alright. Got his nucleic acids at the right spot in the chain, if you know what I mean. Oh, I guess you probably don't. I'll explain later. Let's not get caught up in details, shall we.

"Don't worry about the immune system, Control. We've been inhabiting bats for ages now, so nothing we haven't dealt with before. Just try to stay out of the immune systems sight and move in herds. Don't forget, we're stronger together. Now, let's go get the numbers up. I need everyone to go and get into a cell. Replication is our highest priority at this stage!"

"But sir, I don't have a good feeling about this."

Oh my . . . Control. He's a little bit of a sissy, this one. And how many times have I told him to just call me RoNA?

"Come on, Control. Cells are the smallest unit of structural and functional life. I'm sure you're able to handle one of the others on your own. They make the perfect nesting

spot. Get their protein manufacturing working for us. Do what we do best. Turn them into mindless reproducing robots. You know the drill! Use your molecular arsenal to highjack reproduction, and, if it's a stubborn cell, penetrate it right away. They won't even know what's happening to them. It'll churn out proteins with our genetic code inside. Biohacking at its finest boys! From then on it will be easy-peasy. Also, stop with the sir!"

How rude of me—I think I failed to introduce myself. My name is Lord RoNA Virion, and I'm the head of this bat's corona virus culture. No need for that level of formality, though. You can just call me RoNA. Pleasure to meet you. Wait, just give me one moment—I have to make sure everyone else is in position.

"Alpha Troop, get going! The rookies are taking their sweet time and I need you all to be at the first lymph nodes in ten minutes, tops! Off you go!"

Sorry about that. Where were we? Right, I'm running the show here. Took over this bat from another. Same species, so it was relatively easy to make the jump. They are very sexual animals, you know. It's mating season currently. Don't think it'll be longer than twenty-four hours until my host mates with another, easy-peasy. They are animals, in both the literal and figurative sense.

But I digress. Back to me and the culture. You're probably wondering how we are able to take over whole organisms so efficiently. Well, we're actually all in the same boat, you and us. We all want to ensure our survival. You see, it's nothing personal for us, really.

"OK, everyone, all virions get into position. Yes, and by all virions, I mean all viral cells. Or, in other words, entire virus particles with your proteins and shells and all! You, Delta Troop, I want you to go and infiltrate all the entries and exits in the respiratory system. We need to make sure that when our little, flying, furry chiropteran friend here starts coughing, we can get as many kamikaze viral loads out there as possible. Not everyone is going to make it. We're gonna lose a lot of good viral cells. But don't forget what awaits you if you make it. Yes, that's right. You'll be able to start a new culture in a new organism, like I have."

Well, it basically will be me all over again. You see, since we're all the same, wherever one of my mate virions goes, I go. Like a 'hive-mind', if you will. That basically allows me to also travel between multiple hosts whenever I want. So, don't get confused when I'm suddenly inhabiting different hosts later on.

"But sir!"

"RoNA. I said call me RoNA! Control, how many times do I need to tell you?"

"I'm sorry, sir. I just can't help it. But what about—what about Gravity?"

Uh, Gravity. One of our ancient archnemeses, targeting our virions carried by droplet and aerosol fighters. Gravity, always trying to hold us down, with its heavy blanket of weight, trying to prevent us from spreading through the air. At least these are the kinds of stories and information that our Mother Genome encodes and imprints onto the RNA of our new virus cells as they are being manufactured. You could see it as the base knowledge that every virion is born with. Though Gravity is actually the least of our worries. Those rookies just don't know it yet.

"Recruits, don't worry about Gravity. Those of you being spurted out in droplets, yes, you will be sucked down to the floor. But fear not! I can sense the climate here is warm enough. Once your carrier droplet begins evaporating into the air, it will carry you right back up into our troposphere. So, don't worry, you'll be back up and united with the rest of the aerosols in no time."

"Can't I become an aerosol right away, sir?"

"Out of our control."

No pun intended. Also, in case you are wondering, the troposphere stretches from the sea level all the way up to ten kilometers in height. It's basically the area that most mammals live in.

"Our host specimen coughs on its own. Some particles are larger, 10-20 microns, resulting in droplets, and some are smaller. Anything below 10 microns is considered an

aerosol; it's completely up to chance. Oh, and to give you an example for size comparison, we corona virions are roughly 0.1 microns in diameter and a red blood cell is around 5 microns across, so we are talking invisible to the naked eye. This means that a very large amount of our rookie virions can fit into an aerosol and even more into a droplet."

"Fascinating, sir, but it sounds very dangerous and random."

"Indeed, it is. We virions do live on the edge, in a sense. After all, once we can't find another viable host to survive in, that's it for us. We cough our last breath, so to speak."

"So, sir, are we in danger of not finding another viable host, then?"

He is really of the anxious and conservative kind, isn't he? I remember being cautious, too, when I was young and just hatched out of a cell, but he's a little bit over-the-top scared. I actually can't be bothered with this whole teaching thing, but let's face it, who else is going to do it?

"No, Control, don't worry. We are quite lucky in a sense. We've been inhabiting these bats for a while now and pretty well know our way around them. They are the perfect reservoir hosts for us and other emerging viruses. Bats are actually quite unique. They have characteristics that make them exquisite hosts for viruses and other disease agents, like their choice of food, population structure, their ability to fly and echolocate, seasonal migration patterns, daily

movements, their virus susceptibility (of course), and their very long life span. Some of them can live thirty-five years or more."

Control probably won't understand half of what I'm saying. I am counting on you, however. You better pay attention. I'm usually not one to explain things twice.

"Echolocation and susceptibility, sir?"

Told you. He's not the smartest. I'm feeling tired already by this whole question-game-master dynamic that's going on.

"Hmpf . . . let me elaborate. Bats are one of the most abundant groups of mammals and, except for rodents and some others, they are also the most widely distributed. They live in greatly populated densities and have a very overcrowded roosting behavior. They cluster as tightly together as 300 bats per square foot, in populations of several million individuals. They are the perfect breeding ground for intra- and interspecies transmission of viral infections."

"Wow, no wonder we spread through them so well! They seem to have numbers and densities similar to us!"

"That's right. The structure and demographics of bat populations are very viable for viruses like us. It allows viruses to cause acute and persistently maintained infections. There are usually so many bats in one population

that it's the perfect mixing vessel for viruses and other bacteria."

"I guess that's why they huddle so close together? They can't see properly. Blind as a bat?"

"That's actually not true at all. Most of them have sight, even better eyesight than other mammals. But the even more impressive visual detection method they possess is their echolocation. They are, in fact, the only land mammal that uses this technique. They emit a very intense high-frequency sound that bounces off of objects around it. The bat then detects and analyzes the properties of the echoes to navigate, and it does all this while flying. The sound they emit is extremely loud, so loud it can be deafening for some other mammals. It is emitted through the mouth and the nostrils and is so powerful that small-particle aerosols and droplets of saliva and mucus are ejected. And yes, you guessed it. Those droplets and aerosols are basically a free transport for us to infect other nearby bats and potential hosts."

"So isn't it a little bit overcrowded in terms of virus cultures? With a transmission that works that flawlessly and population numbers that large?"

"Tell me about it, Control. There is an abundance of different viruses, even here in our host. There are some distant and other not-so-distant coronavirus brothers and sisters. But don't worry, they are nothing compared to us. I was supposed to go on a date with rabies yesterday, another

very common one, but I stood her up. So, let me know if you see her coming, I'll have to make for an exit."

"But sir, why did you stand her up?"

"Between the two of us, she's really getting into my head too fast and just, how do I put it, she foams up easily, if you know what I mean?"

"No sir, I don't quite know what you m—"

"She has a fiery temper and gets mad at me too easily."

Seriously, Mother Genome, why have you forsaken me with an emotional, seemingly autistic control cell? Well, this should hopefully be enough for now.

"Control, be a good chap and just instruct the rest of the rookies accordingly please, will ya?"

I hope I don't have to start whipping him later in order to follow through with what I am asking of him. Lazy viruses are the worst. Especially in these busy bat hosts. You need to keep your culture on its toes. Man, I got to say, these bats have been pretty draining. And don't even get me started about how LOUD they are. So loud! I think I'd be ready for a change of species-scenery.

"Yes, sir, I will try my best."

"Thanks, buddy."

I don't want to come across as lazy, but I am ready to take a NAP after this first day of teaching Control. And no, it's not what you think it is. It works in a similar way, yes, but it stands for nucleic acid polymers. Those nucleic acid polymers act in an antiviral way. It can be weakening for me, but in the right quantity, it's the perfect little nightcap, you see. A high-achieving virion lord like myself needs some alone time every once in a while. With everyone asking so many questions all the time, it's hard to shut off, you know? So, I am . . . ah . . . just using this as a little sleeping agent. No big deal. Literally, the doses are very small.

YES, I know, I know exactly what you're thinking. Don't worry, I'm using proper portion control and just very teeny-tiny amounts at a time, just enough for a little sleepy buzz occasionally, if you know what I mean, he-he.

Don't tell Control. I don't want him to freak out or anything. Also, it's not really meant for young virions. It's more of an acquired taste for adult lords, like myself. He won't understand, anyways.

And he's still here, too, isn't' he? He can try taking the reins every now and then when I'm, well, in a higher state. He's a baby still, and has lots to learn, but why not learn by doing it, right?

So where were we? Oh yes, time for my NAP.

Two

The Hunt

Geezus! What was that? Definitely louder than anything else I've heard before. Damn, and we're off flying around again. Oh, wait, something's different though. We're just flying downward? Looks like our host lost control of its motor functions. And here's Gravity, one of our archnemeses, toying with us all again. Interesting, I'm also starting to feel a little tired. Which is weird, because I just had a NAP! Or wait, maybe it's because I just had a NAP! Well, sometimes it's hard to tell if it's the after effect of the NAP or not. But safety first! I better check in with Control. The host might be in some sort of trouble. Good thing that we are able to use our hosts senses as if they were our own, smell, hearing, sight, taste and touch. Control is acting as my eyes and ears while I'm busy. Yes, yes okay, while I sleep. Just don't tell him, alright?

"Control, what do you see and hear coming from the bat's cerebral activity?"

"Nothing, sir. The lights are slowly going out up here. The bat's echolocation is not working anymore. Audio is jagged. The only thing we can make out is that there is some sort of two-legged creature with a long, black tube-like thing walking towards us. I believe they are mammals."

"Oh, that can't be good. We have barely established ourselves well enough to spread to another organism. If we don't act fast, the current host might be a dead-end for us."

"Sir, we just got a report that there is a foreign body that entered our host and hit vital organs. We are slowly shutting down."

Damn, that's the last thing we needed. A host full of rookie virions, low viral numbers in general, and now this? Well, I hope the other cultures are doing better.

"Sir, we are being picked up and loaded into some sort of transportation device. There is an abundance of bats and other hosts in here too. I believe I can make out snakes and penguins. None of them are moving. They are all still, like our host."

Oh dear, he means pangolins. The scaly anteater. I would scold him if we had the time.

"Quick! Try to fire up the respiratory system with what we have left. Maybe we can jump to another host before it's too late."

"Negative, sir. The other organisms around us seem to be in the same shutdown state as we are. Survival chances are low even if we were to successfully make the transmission."

That's not good. There goes our chance of survival by spilling over to other live hosts. Come on, this can't be it. Think! Think, RoNA, there has to be a way out of this. This is the worst—I don't want it to end here, not like this! I am Lord RoNA Virion, and I am . . . "

"Sleepy, sir. I'm feeling sleepy as well now."

Damn it, he is getting weak, me too. I feel like I can't think straight. This shall teach me a lesson not to take another NAP and leave this absolute noob in control! Ah! I have an idea.

"Control, what about the two-legged mammal commanding the transportation device? Could we reach it?"

"Negative, sir. It seems to be sheltered behind some sort of invisible material. In addition to that, there are also wind gusts working against us, carrying our virions the other way. We're losing them by the minute. Sir, how much time do we have left?"

Isn't he funny? Some invisible material? Not sure what he's talking about, but the more I listen, the more I think that he took some of my NAP as well, haha. Oh man, those young viral assistants are just SO much work to build up and get to an autonomous level. If it only would have taken more charge of everything prior to those two-legged mammals showing up. Don't you dare point fingers and give me that look. I told you, I'm having trouble turning my brain off without the NAP. Okay, calm down, think. I better get back to Control. Ah, I might be onto something.

"Hmm, hard to say. Let me think. In theory, it all depends on what our viral composition is. What did Mother Genome

say again? Ah yes, environmental temperatures, humidity and location of the viral cells can impact inactivation of viral materials. For example, which organ and how the host is disposed of plays a big role. The bad news for us is that unlike bacteria who can grow on their own, we cannot. We need a living host with living cells to replicate our genetic material. The question is, how long will it take for all of our virions to cease their infectiousness? It's not like flipping a switch once a host dies. We don't just all suddenly die. In order for us virions to move our genome from cell to cell, we need protection from the environment. There are usually two pathways for us to do so. The first one is for us virions to surround our genome with a double-layered shell made out of fat that we steal from other cells that we have highjacked. These viruses are called enveloped viruses. The second way is for us to build a spherical shell of proteins, forming the round and spiky-looking corona armor that we usually all carry around us. These types of virions are our close cousins. They are called capsid viruses."

No, we're not going out just like that.

"Control, do we still have a grip on what the temperature and humidity might be? Also, have the enzymatic juices started flowing?"

"Negative, sir. But to our recollection, before our host fell down to the floor, moderately humid and warm."

Hmm . . . As for humid versus dry environments, we should be fine. For the majority of viruses, especially the enveloped type like ourselves, drier environments can lead to faster times of inactivation.

"Ok, Control, stay on standby for now. We will just have to wait it out and see where we and our little bat host are being led. And please, how many more times do I need to tell you? Stop calling me sir."

The transport seems to be coming to a halt. It has also been getting less bumpy. It should still be nightfall, yet Control keeps reporting that there are a lot of lights outside. Oh, we've stopped completely now. There is nothing else left, other than the vibration of the transportation device. Okay, I guess our best chance now is to try to get onto this two-legged mammal. Whatever it takes.

"Ok, everyone in position! The more contact we get to the two-legged mammals, the better. Be ready to enter any cut, wound, or airway you can find. Make sure to get onto their paws and claws if possible."

Interesting, we are being brought into a place with a lot of these two-legged mammals and what seems to be a very diverse range of other inactive animal hosts. Well, our journey might not be over just yet. I've encountered different mammals before and something feels familiar about them. Impossible to tell what they are really like and how they behave, though.

"Boys, get ready! Control tells me that there are quite a few different species out there."

"But sir, we won't be able to jump over to—"

"No recruits. That's right. We're not meant to jump over to different species. You all know what this means. We will have to go zoonotic. It will be hard. Between us and survival, there are a number of potential new immune systems, antibodies, and other complementary defense systems, like the spleen, thymus, and even bone marrow. Remember what the genome taught each and every one of you when you were created: you are survival machines, engineered to take over and reproduce. We will do what we do best—ensure our survival."

"Yes, sir!"

"Everyone ready! Boost viral loads into fluid channels. Alpha and Beta Team, disperse between the interstitial, intravascular, transcellular, and intracellular fluid. Get it flowing, boys."

"Affirmative, sir. Confirming the infusion of viral loads into blood vessels, fluids between cells, and other small channels throughout the body."

Three

Change of Species-Scenery

Excellent! Everyone is deployed and ready to go. Now we just wait.

"Control, what is the situation like out there?"

"More and more two-legged mammals, sir. They are everywhere. Their numbers are so abundant. If I didn't know any better, I'd say they are part of a virus themselves!"

"Hah! What should we name them? Any suggestions?"

"There seems to be a lot of chatter and some biochemical code written on signs and flat surfaces. The two-leggers keep pronouncing it as 'human.'"

"Humans? Sounds like mutant! I like them already. Remember what Mother Genome always said? The key to going zoonotic is mutation. Nomen est omen. Haha!"

Perfect! Now it will be a question of time. I know our chances are low, but one thing we won't do for certain is give up. All we have to do is get in touch with a new host organism and break down the barrier between them and us. Or, in other words (as mentioned earlier), go full zoonotic. Yes, I know, once we make it into a new organism, we still have to overcome the local defense mechanisms, and the chance of making it is low, but we have got to try. The next step after we manage to evade the immune system is to breach the membrane of a cell. Most cells are covered with certain receptors that won't allow us to interact with them. It's like a secret handshake we need to master first. We've been in other similar mammals before, so I have a strong feeling that the ACE2 receptor will be our gateway in. It is the most vulnerable receptor within other mammals like cats, ferrets, and pigs. Chances are our little mutants—oh, I mean humans—might just share the same receptor. This might be our way inside. Worth a try!

Aaaaand jackpot!

"Control, I can sense we just have been picked up. What's happening outside?"

"Positive, sir. We are being carried to some sort of station where hosts get disassembled. There could be an opportunity for spillage for us."

"Spreadtastic! To all viral loads: get ready to dispatch in case of separation from limbs or other body parts."

What was that I just heard? That must have been one limb flying off in separation. Great, it begins. Now, you, don't forget what I mentioned earlier: I am the main virion, which is just a fancy word for saying an entire virus particle in all its glory. And yes, what a glory indeed. Whichever of my recruits manages to spillover, we will automatically be travelling with them. Wherever they (I don't want to call them my children, even though they sort of are) go, I go through and with them. I've been pretty busy; there are a few million copies of me, or, as I like to call them, the culture. I do have to say that all these years within bats has made me quite curious to explore a different species. These bats are a made bed, but it's been getting a bit monotonous, to be honest.

"Control? Have we been separated already from certain body parts? . . . Control?!"

I see, they must have separated him off already. I will regress at this point to save energy and wait for one of my children—ahem . . . I mean copies—to successfully enter a new organism. Fingers crossed. And no, don't worry, I'm not taking another NAP at this point. I need to stay sharp. This is quite a critical situation for us, as you can imagine. I will stay away from it until I deserve one again.

Four

New Beginning

What time is it? I feel like I've been knocked out for days. It seems to be dark still. Quiet, yet again. Maybe this is the afterlife? Maybe we didn't make it. Maybe I am all alone now? Maybe I overdosed on the last NAP I took? Perhaps this is it? Well, if it is, I just wanted to tell you about that one time when—

"Sir?"

"Aah, Control!"

"Affirmative, sir! This is Control. We have s—"

"Successfully entered and invaded a new host organism! Well done, everyone. What happened?"

"We got ingested, sir. We spilled over onto a few different other dead hosts, and some of them got ingested by these humans. Most of our mates didn't make it, but there was one that did. And here we are."

Oh my God, yes! Memo to self, this screams for a victory NAP later. Well deserved, I might say. Without my doing, constant training, and supervision, these rookies never would have made it. As much as Control is a novice, he did okay. My precccioussss . . . NA . . . Ahem. Oh, you are still listening? God, don't scare me like that, a little privacy? May I?

"Fantastic! Status report?"

"The human is asleep, it seems, or resting at least. Temperature and vitals are normal. We dispatched some additional virions that made the transport through the intestinal tract alive to the lymphatic system according to protocol."

"Excellent, Control. Don't forget to dispatch virions to the capillaries, the perfect gateway into the organism's circulation. They are the highway of the of the human body and connection points between veins, arteries, and other tissue material."

A new night, a new site! Okay, let's see how hard we can crank the reproduction in one of these humans, shall we? Culture is everything, my friend! As soon as the virion numbers in our new host start to rise, we will be back to feeling as cultured as always!

"How about we settle ourselves in the respiratory tract? I have a good feeling about this one. Sprinkle a little dry cough onto our little human and let the magic happen. First thing's first, though: we need to establish a base. Most importantly, we need to make sure that we don't trigger the immune system's heat defense system, the fever. We don't want to have it heat up our environment and, well, have it raise the temperature to the challenge."

Ah, I can feel movement. I guess it's time to wake up. That's good. Increased cell activity will also increase our reproduction. We also don't want to get our specimen chained to the bed too quickly, that would limit our chances of spreading while we are active inside of him.

"Control, what should we call him?"

"Sir, I believe the specimen had some sort of celebration. There is something in front of him. It's round with spore- and spike-like things coming out of it. He is eating it. There is a name written in between: J-A-M-E-S."

Hah! Interesting! James. Sounds almost like germs. I guess they are not so different from us after all.

"Sir, he's on the move again. I believe he is putting some protective layers of fats on himself. It must be some sort of armor, perhaps the same as the fats we use to shield ourselves against threats?"

"Perhaps. But that theory is yet to be tested."

"He is leaving his nesting spot. We are making our way down through a twisted vein-like corridor. It's rather jagged. Sir, we are getting into another one of those transportation vehicles. What if he also goes to one of those places where his limbs get separated off. Should we be concerned?"

"Calm down. Let's just see what happens next. Given what happened at this place yesterday, I have a strong feeling that they don't eat their own kind. I saw a lot of different animal species yesterday across all those plates, but no humans. What was surprising, though, was that there was such a variety of animal species present. They must be eating

everything! If it were not a high-risk place for us to be, I would suggest hanging around there more often. Plenty of spillage opportunity, it seems."

But back to the here and now. It's clear now that these humans use these transport devices to get from A to B. Maybe some out-of-body lymphatic system?

"Sir, another human just joined the transport."

"What are they doing? Is one trying to attack or infiltrate the other?"

"No, sir. The other human is just sitting silently in the back of the transport. Odd."

Maybe there is some invisible transaction happening, hidden from what we can see through his eyes? The situation yesterday at the place with all the dead hosts clearly showed that they are social; they are bound to have an interaction sooner or later. Let's wait a couple of minutes.

"Sir, the human in the back just gave our host something and left. Shortly after, another human came and joined the transport. He was talking, but not to our host; it was to someone else who is entirely invisible to us."

"Elaborate?"

"I believe they can talk to others while not being in the same physical place."

Fascinating. So they are using a similar communication basis to ours? Perhaps similar to the way you and I talk? And could it be that our host is responsible for transporting others in this lymphatic system for some kind of reimbursement? Maybe he is able to upgrade his armor with more fats.

It's been a few hours now, nonstop, the same cycle all over again. Another human gets in, leaves something to our host, and then gets out again. How dull.

"Control, how is our Alpha Troop doing in the respiratory system?"

"Reports say they are slowly establishing ourselves, sir. It won't be long before the body starts to slowly engage in dry cough and a sore throat."

"Excellent! That means that soon we will have a higher chance of our viral loads travelling farther to different hosts."

"Sir, we are heading back into his nest, I believe."

"Good, that gives us some time to further grab a foothold in his system. Tomorrow is another day."

How convenient that there is this thing constantly blowing cold, fresh air on top of us? Amazing, these humans and their systems! It's keeping us from overheating—beautiful. Well, what more can I say? A very successful new invasion of not only a new host but a new species all together. This cries for an after-work NAP. I know what you're thinking: I'm taking too many. But I can guarantee you this is all under control and there is no such thing as abusive behavior with virions. I mean, yes, we do abuse other cells in order to replicate, so to speak, but that's different altogether. Do as I do! Relax and take a NAP or whatever it is that gets you off.

"Sir? . . . Sir? . . . Lord RoNA Virion, sir?"

Oh damn, how long was I out? Has he been calling me for long?

"I'm here, Control, I'm here. What's up?"

"Sir, I have been trying to get in touch with you for four days! We have managed to fully develop the early stages of the sore throat and dry cough."

Four DAYS? Ah, no I don't need you to tell me "I told you so." I get it, okay? I probably took too big of a NAP. Those nucleic acid polymers must be getting more potent. Okay, okay, I took too much. I'll be more careful. Let's just leave it at that. Now, what's happening. Oh, a dry cough? Great. He's not so useless after all, that Control, is he? Seems like we are settled in this host for good now. Well established. There is no getting rid of us at this point, not even with an all-powerful immune system. A fever could become dangerous, but let's see if it even gets triggered. This is fantastic, though! When the culture thrives, I thrive. Ecstatic is an understatement. Control has taken more charge and can be trusted more. More importantly, though, he did it all without me having to attend to him and guide him around the clock.

"Control, you've done well. I got a little surprise for you, since you've been working on James's symptoms so hard. We are about to head out!"

"Thank you, sir! Symptastic!"

Pff . . . Symptastic? Really? Just when I'm about to think that he deserves praise and that he's coming out of his shell, he turns uncool like that? Oh well, I guess you can teach them young ones, but you can't teach them class, style, and wit. Well, at least he seems to be using the time well when I'm out.

I'd love to stick around, James, but something happened over night and my guidance is needed somewhere else. Recruits of ours managed to travel into a different nest through the white box that keeps sucking and blowing air into our host's nest. It seems to be connected to different human nests. Like a multifold lung. I believe Control identified the box as something called 'Ducted Air Condition Mujitsu DX-12.' This might be another secret way humans travel. Fascinating.

"Control, let's go! We got another site to attend."

"But sir, I forgot to ask, how? And what about Jam—"

"He will be sick even without our constant attention. The rest of the virions we leave behind will make sure to increase their numbers throughout the next few days. Chances are good that he will transfer our virions to other humans all on his own. No need for the two of us to stick around. I can tell

you exactly what's going to happen. He seems reasonably healthy, not too old, and his immune system is mainly intact. If you were to fast forward ten days, not much else would happen. The symptoms will most likely result in further sore throat and a dry cough. His body is too healthy to develop more serious symptoms like pneumonia. Even though I LOVE a good pneumonia. Or, how I like to call it—lung party! It's an infection that causes his air sacs in his lungs to become inflamed. Those sacs are also called alveoli. They will fill with fluid or pus, making it difficult to breathe. We viruses are expert cell manipulators. We are able to change to existing cells in his lung sacs and clog them up. Goblet cells that produce mucus and silica cells which have hairs on them usually prevent the lungs from flooding. We are able to combine those two cells together like a sweet, tangy cocktail and flood the lungs. It's sooo much fun! Everyone is gobbling down goblets, as you can imagine. There's not much he'd be able to do, unless he has one of those Mujitsu blowers to keep pushing air into his lungs—that might dry them out again. Another more serious condition that can result from the lung party, I mean pneumonia, is that if we keep pushing the immune system it might fail, and that would lead to further organ damage and death. But again, very unlikely with him, and thus quite boring. Even though the slightest chance of binding and firing up those goblet cells for a drink gets me excited!"

"But sir, how are we transmitting our virions to the next host?"

"Can't feel it yet? I can sense that a few of our virions successfully invaded an older female days ago. Some virions were able travel early on through the DX-12 air blower into the next nesting place just behind these walls."

"Whoa, sir! But h—"

"Let's move on! No time to waste! I can't wait to see what our next host is like. Nothing personal, germs, I mean James. Byeeee."

I have to admit, this is getting more and more exciting, seeing what this species is like. It's quite complex, yet not very sophisticated in some ways. I can't wait to see what happens next.

I'm off to that new female specimen. See you there!

Five

Mother Genome

This female specimen is up way earlier than James. I wonder why. It is still dark outside.

"Control, what's happening out there? What is she doing?"

"She seems to be preparing something to eat. She keeps separating things with a device similar to the ones humans used to separate the bat's body parts. She also keeps ingesting small pieces every now and then on random occasions."

"I see. Maybe she is about to devour something large."

"Sir, there is another smaller male human. He just entered the space. His eyes are barely open. He's starting to eat."

"Interesting, maybe we will be able to spread through what he is eating, like we did a few days ago."

"Yes, perhaps. Sir, can I ask you a question? How did we travel through the DX-12 Unit?"

"Remember when I told the new recruits on day one about aerosols? James must have developed a dry cough overnight and started coughing out aerosols. Basically, particles smaller than 10 microns can travel through the air quite a bit farther than droplets, defying the force of gravity

for a little bit longer. Aerosols can even be carried by winds and streams in the air. I believe that we managed to slip into whatever they call 'air-conditioning' and came out here on the other end."

"Crazy! Full of surprises, this human world."

"Indeed, Control, indeed."

"Sir, the little human seems to have finished eating. They seem to call this function 'breaky.' Maybe it's to strengthen themselves like creatures do in the animal kingdom? The younger male human just put on additional layers of protection before he left."

"I wonder if he is another transport master like James."

Ok, let's not get sidetracked. Before we get to explore this new human, we need to make sure we are able to stick around. We need to keep establishing ourselves here in this adult female before we get to further enjoy the show on the outside. Since this host is more mature than our previous one, the immune system might try some different tricks on us. Data indicates that her body temperature is already slowly rising. Not necessarily a good sign. We should keep tabs on that. If this continues, she might fall ill more quickly than we expected. Among other symptoms like the dry cough manifested by James, she might also get tired, even though she seems to be quite a tireless specimen, organizing her nest, which is very unlike James's space, after the smaller human left. I am very curious to see how this female's body defends itself differently than James's. If I had to guess, I'd assume that eventually she will experience aches and pains, a sore throat, headaches, diarrhea, and maybe a loss of taste and smell for a certain period of time. Even serious symptoms like difficulty breathing, pressure in her chest, and pain and loss of speech movement. But I am even more curious to see what behavioral differences there are between James and her.

"She really does seem tireless. Control, what is she doing now?"

"She is still organizing her nest. Not quite sure why she does certain things, like fold other unused pieces of protective layers and stow them away. I don't quite understand. She also made some sort of documentation earlier."

"Maybe she's is trying to count something."

"Perhaps. Does she also get the same form of remuneration as James for all the work she is doing in her nest?"

"It does not seem like it, sir. I think it's also due to the fact that there is no one around to witness it."

"Why is she doing it, then? If she doesn't get anything in remuneration and nobody seems to be thanking her?"

"Odd indeed, sir. I think we are about to head out. Good chance to aim for another spillover. What do you think, sir?"

"Exactly my thinking, Control. How are we doing in terms of viral loads in her throat, nose, and the rest of the respiratory system?"

"Looking good, sir. Climbing steadily. We can see that her body is feeling the toll more quickly than James's. Despite her energy depleting at a faster rate, she is pushing on."

"I like to hear that! Another feature quite like our own."

Don't let yourself get outpaced; if you want to survive, you got to push through even if it is hard at times.

"Sir, our host has left the nest now. We are outside. There seems to be an abundance of other humans just lingering around on the pathways. They might not belong to a nest. They also lack protective layering, like our host. Their eyes keep following us. It's bizarre. They seem to be hurt and not quite alright."

"Hmm. Not quite sure what those humans on the floor are doing, but they seem quite lost and helpless. None of the other humans seem to care for them much. As if they are outcast. Can you imagine us outcasting certain virions? Not supporting our recruits and other RNA carriers and just leaving them to themselves? Barbaric."

"Sir, our host just gave one of those on the ground a few pieces of something. The same thing that James received in the transport."

"Interesting. So they also give each other things without any sort of remuneration? I wonder why James does not just sit out here instead?"

"Sir, sir! I think I know what the small pieces of remuneration are for. It must be a form of credit. I just saw some humans trading it for protective layers in a well-lit place full of identical looking 'c-l-o-t-h-i-n-g' (I believe they call it)."

"Ha, I see. So they use it as a way of enhancing themselves. We seem to be right, it does act as protective fat layers do. I wonder if the human on the ground will enhance himself too with the credit he received."

"Well, he'd better, because guess what? We managed to get some of our recruits onto the credits that the female host passed on to the human on the floor."

"Actually, sir, the human on the floor was already infected. I remember him now. He was one of the passengers in James's transport. Shocking how his appearance has changed so quickly. And why does he cower on the floor now?"

"Ah, sure . . . I knew that this is the same human of course."

Interesting observation, indeed. Impressive that Control caught on, maybe not a dud after all. There seems to be some sort of hierarchy going on within the human world. And it might all be based on how much credit one has to buy themselves more protective layering. At least that's the only way that I can explain it right now.

"Sir, what about the little human belonging to the female host?"

"You haven't noticed yet?"

"You saying we already infiltrated him?"

"Yes, indeed, we did infiltrate him. We managed to get him two ways even! We had recruits placed on what he ate and in addition to that we also had aerosols in the air. They went straight down his lung."

"Impressive, sir. You never cease to amaze me. Also, I saw him watching something earlier on a flickering panel. It was chattering. He was looking at it all the way through 'breaky' and he was talking about 't-i-k t-o-k-s' that go viral? Sir, did he know when we infiltrated his body because he was talking about virals? Are 't-i-k t-o-k-s' some new form of aerosol?"

"Viral? Very odd. Usually organisms don't know when we infiltrate them. And 't-i-k t-o-k-s?' Never heard about it. Maybe some new all-powerful micro and soft virus?"

"Sir, why are we not exploring the younger ones?"

"Their immune systems seem to be too strong for us. The one that we saw earlier was not very susceptive to potential symptoms. He definitely has our virions; they are reproducing inside of him. However, he most likely won't show any severe symptoms. The transmission rate is also

lower. This is probably because most of them are asymptomatic."

"Asymptomatic, sir?"

"Yes, you see, it means that he is infected, but he does not display any or most of the symptoms that we would usually see in a different species or a different human. Some symptoms are quite important for us in order to spread. If you look, for example, at James's dry cough. If he hadn't developed it, we might never have been able to travel into the female host through the—I still can't believe it—Mujitsu DX-12! The young human will still spread our virions, but what gets me excited are the symptoms. Since he won't show many, let's not waste our time bothering with low-priority specimens like him.

"Fascinating. How we are able to spread through all sorts of airways and surfaces, sir."

"Yes, indeed. For example, we are able to survive quite a while on surfaces. We can easily survive on plastic for as long as seventy-two hours after placing our recruits on it. Around twenty-four hours on steel and cardboard and up to four hours on copper—so stay away from that stuff."

"Why copper specifically, sir?"

"Most heavy metals, like gold and silver, are antibacterial. But copper is a bit different. It is comprised of a very specific atomic structure"

Giving it kryptonite-like powers against us and other pathogens, or, in other words, microorganisms that can cause diseases.

"It has an additional free electron in its outer orbital shell made of electrons that take part in oxidation. You could say it becomes a molecular oxygen bomb."

"Wow, we are almost unstoppable! So what could humans do to shield themselves against us, other than wear their protective layering? Layer up with copper?"

"Let's not talk about copper anymore, please. It gives me the willies. Unfortunately there are, however, a few things they can do. Even though I hate to talk about it, I guess it's only fair that you know what our death might look like. Firstly, they could isolate themselves. If we can't jump onto a new host within a given amount of time or before the immune system gets rid of us, that's our end. Another way of getting rid of us is to use soap. I am sure humans must have developed similar things, since they occur naturally in nature in animal fats and plant oil. I have a few cousins that were wiped out by accident that way. Remember how I told you about enveloped and capsid viruses? Enveloped viruses use lipids, or fats, to shield themselves against attacks from the immune system. Unfortunately, fats are more sensitive to the environment and tend to have more difficulty surviving than capsids. Enveloped viruses fall victim to drying out and are more sensitive to other disinfectant solutions than

capsids. That is also why soap, and simply washing surfaces with it, protects against us. See, soap has a lot of lipids, or fats, in it too. The fats from the soap find a way in between the fats of our protective envelope and manage to break it apart, inactivating our virions, meaning they are suppressing our actions by altering our form or environment."

"Oh, that was . . . a lot. I wish I never asked. Hey, sir, there are some flickering panels around and behind our host. I just saw an orange-haired human in blue protective layering telling other humans to eat soap and something called 'sanitizer.' That can't be good."

"Yes, Control, that does not sound good. In fact, it will most likely kill our host before it even reaches us. Damn it, orange-haired human, be smarter! Do not destroy all these valuable hosts for us! Come on, they must have a better trump card than this."

"Sir, I have to say, I wish we were a capsid virus, to be honest."

"I hear you, Control."

Well, there are pros and cons to everything in life. I was introduced to another capsid years ago through a friend of a friend. Her name is Ebola. We could ask her about what her life is like, but she is probably busy. I think she is currently trying to avoid paying off the bill to the gates of her extinction. But that is a story for another time . . .

Six

Life on the Edge

I am curious. What could have happened to our new host that it transitioned from being able to pay James for transport to living outside on the street within a matter of days? The hierarchy among humans linked to this credit they are dealing with must be very competitive and steep. Assuming they are all trying to achieve a goal similar to the one we are, survival, they seem to be running a very limited and flawed system to support their communities. This host is deteriorating by the minute and does not show much strength to prevail against us. I personally don't care for this host or any other, but I do care about our own survival, and for that we need to be able to reproduce and spread. I don't want to play the blame game, but the humans are cutting us off on this one.

I almost feel sorry for this one here, all alone on the streets . . . but then again . . . nah! I really just have one goal. It's not personal.

"Control. It's time. GET READY TO PAAAARTAYYY! Tell our troops to go and start binding goblet and silica cells in his lungs, because it is pneumonia time. We need to get this one into a place where there is more traffic with other

humans to infect. Crank the viral loads in the respiratory system."

"Understood, sir. We've successfully dispatched the majority of our virions into his lungs. Like we've seen happening to others, it should be a matter of days before we get picked up by one of the blue blinking transports. Sir, it's just very confusing how some humans are treated differently than others. It's a mystery, really."

"Now, now, Control. Let's not get sentimental about them. We are mere spectators en route trying to survive. It is not our responsibility to care for them or make exceptions. We are doing what we do best. We—"

"We survive, sir, I know. I guess you were right earlier when you were saying that that we and the humans are quite alike."

Oh, he's turning into a softy now? Still won't call me by my preferred name, but he is becoming empathetic towards humans. Also, what's with his cutting me off? Is he for real? Well, that's almost too much drama for one day for me. I will ponder how to tackle this . . . Oh, who am I kidding? I'm going to doze off and maybe just have teeny-tiny NAP. I promise this will be the last one. Guaranteed. Maybe you, too, should have one. Well, whatever you do, make sure not to do it on copper.

Seven

All Cells Matter

"Sir! Sir!"

"What's up, Control? I'm up, I'm up!"

See? Told you a small NAP won't do anything. I TOTALLY have it under control.

"There it was again, that loud sound that we also heard before our bat host was captured. Large numbers of humans seem to be running towards it. We are in a different host already. Another human came by yesterday and gave us some more credit, though not enough to change our social status. We remained on the street. A lot of protective clothing in sight, yet unreachable. I took it upon myself to have some virial loads dispatched into the air in aerosols through a few well-placed coughs and we made it. We are in a new host now. And ah, he's different."

"Ah, well done, Control. Glad to be woken up to such exciting news. Come again? What do you mean he is different?"

"His complexion is different. He is darker than the other humans we inhabited before. I would almost say he is as black as the bat."

"So? Any differences internally we should be aware of? Status report."

"No, sir, no differences internally whatsoever. Just purely the color."

"Well, in that case, we shall not judge. A new host, a new protein cell to invade, and an immune system to evade. Control, what is all that rummaging about on the outside?"

"I can't quite explain it, sir. It seems that a group of white humans have eliminated one of the black ones, the same color as our host."

"On purpose?"

"It seems so."

"What a waste! A potential host destroyed? For what reason?"

"Not sure, sir. It seems like the colored humans are investigating and accumulating in large masses on their networks. Transports are being blocked from driving and loud noises are appearing everywhere."

It's a mystery. Why do these humans do what they do? I am sure they must have had a very good reason for not only reducing their own species but for also limiting our chances of spreading. Outrageous. They surely wouldn't do it just because of optical appearances. They are internally the same, exactly like our report states. If anything, they might be differently colored because of a mutation that occurred. And, of course, we all know mutations can be for the better, like when we mutate. They should be worshipping the dark ones!

Maybe give them a special crown or something, like a panther helmet? I don't know, you tell me. Get creative.

"Sir, what could have led them to attack the colored human? Are we in danger in this host? Should we consider returning to a brighter one?"

"You know what I thought about, Control? I just reflected on what could have caused the attack. It might just be something inherent not just to cells and genes but also to humans. Selfishness."

"Selfishness, sir?"

"Yes, Control. Let me tell you about genes and their selfishness. You probably heard about them: TP53, TNF, EGFR, and so on belong to the most common genes known to humans and viruses today. And between the two of us, TNF and EGFR are real buttheads. But according to some theories, genes can be inherently selfish. And guess what? They make up everything, including our cells and the cells of those we invade. And if you now think about the fact that every human being on this earth is made up of cells, they are essentially all being controlled by—you guessed it—genes. The theory goes as follows."

Believe me when I say this, I've learned it the hard way, genes can be selfish bastards.

"Think about the idea of animal behavior. Whether completely selfish or altruistic, it is under the spell of genes in a secondary, but still very powerful, way. These genes are

doing nothing less than programming beings and dictating their most vital and basic functions. They also might have a certain influence over behavior. The brain, of course, plays a role, too. Most in-the-moment decisions and ad hoc situations are guided by the central nervous system, aka the brain. But you could say that genes are the policy makers and that the brain the final executor. However, in the evolution of the human species specifically, the brain developed itself into a more complex and sophisticated organ. So, it took over the reins in the policy making as well. It is capable of running simulations internally and coming up with optional pathways forward. Logically you could say that the genes got to a point where they saw that the brain is smart enough to take care of all those moment-to-moment decisions and the genes instructed it with one final concluding policy: to do whatever it believes best to keep the organism alive. There are genes within the human body that have not changed for tens and hundreds of millions of years. You see, the difference between a successful, selfish gene and an unselfish gene really matters in evolution. The specimens that are geared toward making a decision that is self-serving have higher chances of survival. And survival, in this sense, means replication. The destiny of the genetically encoded information of genes and their instructions is essentially linked to the fate of the organism or body it resides in."

"Whoa, sir! These humans are very advanced. They can trade credit for new genes. I've seen it! Another place to trade credits for genes! Humans put it on their two legs!"

I am sure he didn't understand and I am very sure that there is no place to just obtain genes, but I am not going to call him out.

"So, sir, you are saying that genes are selfish and that they are the smallest building blocks that make up all living organisms, thus the organism itself will tend to showcase selfish behavior?"

Oh, shocker! He seems to have gotten it.

"Ah, yes . . . Control. That's right. This might be a possible solution for why the other host got eliminated."

Well, talk about teaching new tricks to old dogs . . . or young . . . ? Well, I am sure you know what I mean.

"Control, can you take over for a second? I'll be busy for a little bit. All this pondering and diving into selfishness has rubbed off on me. I'd like some alone time."

Or should I say selfish time?

"No problem, sir! I'll hold position and make sure to stay on track on organism expansion within this less selfish colored human."

Well, that's not exactly how I meant it, but yeah. Ah . . . I do have this itch . . . this itch for a . . . ah . . . okay, can you just not judge me? I am taking a NAP. It is the last one. Just relax. Control is so well versed now in what to do that it's all good. A little bit of time apart also won’t hurt, I’m sure. He’s been getting cockier lately, anyways, so maybe he’ll calm down if I just leave him for a few hours.

Eight

Credits and Protective Layers

"Sir, are you there? I think I have a surprise for you."

"Hello, this is Lord Virion. I'm unavailable to take your call right now. Please leave me a message after the—"

"Sir!?"

"Control, relax. I am here. That's just something I heard earlier when the mother human was on the phone. What's up?"

"Ah, good. Well, I got a surprise for you. Please have a look outside."

"Whoa, Control! How did you pull that off?"

I mean, I wish he would have told me his plans beforehand. I am technically the one in command here, so he really should have all of his plans go through me first.

"Control, next time, be so kind as to tell me your plans beforehand, will ya?"

"Yes, sir, of course, apologies. We managed to transfer some virion particles onto someone wearing very nice-looking protective layering coming out of a very shiny building. All it took was the touch of his hand to the hand of our host. I have to say, I cannot claim credit for this, it happened by accident. The new host then touched his face

with his hand and—may I say—BAM! We were in! Can you believe it? Isn't this fantastic?"

BAM? Is that . . . confidence arising in Control? Seems like he is finally letting go of his conservative mindset. What can I say? I'm a teacher of knowledge and life. Although, I must admit, I don't like him continuously acting on his own and swapping hosts just like that. I mean, it is still I, Lord RoNA Virion, who calls the shots, right?

"This is amazing, Control. So this is what it's like for a human with a lot of credits, I assume. His nest looks so shiny and nice. There is also so much space! Oh, and of course our beloved highway between nests—he has one of these air-conditioning units, an aerosol's dream come true."

Heavenly, human-made freeways for us to travel between their nesting spots.

"Say, Control, how is this one doing? He seems to be experiencing an elevated body temperature already. I see the young recruits are fighting a nearly feverish condition? How come this happened so quickly?"

"I've been trying to contact you for a while. You . . . ah . . . have been 'resting' for quite some time. We've already been here for six days."

WHAT? Oh well, I guess I took that selfish gene talk a little too close to heart . . .

"I . . . ah . . . I wasn't resting for that long. Obviously. I was . . . uh . . . observing you and checking in on you

occasionally. You just didn't know it. So it was a test! And you passed. Congratulations. Things did not veer out of, well, control."

"Yes, sir. Sure. Thank you."

"I mean, of course I know all this because I've been observing you over the last six days. But, as another exercise for you, give me a report on how we and our human friend here are doing. It's good practice for you to give official reports, even if I already know everything that will be in the report. I see you've changed back to a white model? Safe is safe, huh?"

"Yes, sir. Well, it was by chance, like I said earlier, but you already know that, I guess. His name is Rich, which apparently is short for Richard. They also converted our name into an abbreviation. I've seen it on the glowing panels."

"Oh yeah? What is it?"

"You won't like it, sir."

"Spit it out, Control!"

"It's covid-19."

"That's a disgrace. It's Lord RoNA Virion to them and nothing else!"

"Yes, your highness, I will make sure to . . . uh . . . pass it on."

"Well, tell me more about this Rich."

"He is quite interesting and different in his social behaviors compared to others, sir. He is clearly higher up in the human hierarchy. I believe he has a lot of credit."

"How come?"

"We successfully infected most of his respiratory system. He is showing a variety of symptoms and has not left his place for days. Very unlike the female mother human we inhabited. He is quite relaxed and seems to enjoy a recurring influx of credit. He even gives credit to another human every day to come and organize his place, like the maternal human did."

"Fascinating. So he enjoys a completely different lifestyle. Very different from the human on the streets. He has a luxurious life and is not dependent on credit handouts like some others?"

"Yes, sir. On the contrary, sir. Even though according to the information panel the world's credits are suffering greatly and have been going through a severe devaluation, Rich is enjoying a prosperous and constant increase of credits. When he is on his communication device, he talks about some sort of 'online business' and 'online sales.' From what I could gather, it's an invisible place where humans spend credit without receiving anything immediately. Very strange."

"Ah, I see history is repeating itself again. Now that I think about it, a very distant ancestor of mine—I can't quite

remember, but I believe last time I heard about him he was in Spain in 1918—also caused some sort of record credit devaluation. I wonder if we are able to take that title from him. I think his name was Hansi or Hinsi. Oh, wait, it was H1N1. That's right. Very successful, that one."

"Yes, sir. Indeed. It is very strange how we, so small and basically invisible, are able to interrupt this global human credit system. Even though it seems very unfair and incorrect, it does seem to hold complexity beneath it."

"Yes, that's quite right, Control. What do they say, again? Oh yeah. 'Small, but oh my!'"

"The imparity between Rich and others, they call them poor humans, is astounding, sir. The flowing-information panel box has been talking almost nonstop over the last six days. Apparently, in order to get credit like James or Rich, one needs a job. Basically, you do something for someone else and then you get credit. And the more credit you have, the better. People that can work from anywhere, like Rich, can stay at home and make sure that they get better. They can rest and relax. But other people, especially the ones that earn less credit, need to always be at a specific place."

"Like James?"

"Yes, exactly like James. If those people don't show up for their jobs, they get no credit."

"So, that means that all the ones that we've made sick over the past weeks and months can't earn credit?"

"Yes, sir. Exactly. According to the chatter box, as we, the virus, spread across the world, we appear to be kickstarting a terrible feedback loop in conjunction with another of the most significant forces of our time: economic inequality. In areas and societies where we and our virions spread, we intensify the ramifications of inequality. Many of which are put onto the losers of today's already over-polarized economies and labor markets. Research proposes that humans on the lower end of the economic layer are more likely to get infected with, well, with us, and then also spread it farther."

Amazing! Praise Mother Genome and the selfishness of humans and their interesting, intricate, and unequal system of wealth and power distribution. Hear! Hear!

"But sir, there is even more."

Wow, look at him! Going off on a rant. The usually 'oh-so-quiet' Control. But who am I kidding? He's definitely changed. I better have a word with him soon. I don't want this to turn into a hostile work environment. I don't want no competition at work, ok? He needs to know his place.

"There are also secondary effects. There are places like schools, where young humans are thought to do certain things."

Ah, yet again, humans are a lot like us. This place sounds like a replication center, like the cells we are using to crank out millions of our own copies. Wondrous!

"Those schools, however, are being closed due to us, covid-1—"

"Control! Don't you dare!"

"Sorry, sir. I mean they are closed due to us, Lord RoNA Virion's survival machine."

That's more like it.

"Many young humans have parents that are part of a low-income group. They are relying on subsidized school lunches and 'breakys' for their daily nutrition. At the same time, their parents most likely won't be able to afford day care, if it is even open. Suddenly, their young ones are home all day."

Excellent! They can spread us around the house.

"Now schools are trying to shift to a virtual online learning plan. However, millions of households are lacking high speed internet, so they might be out of luck. Sir, I'm not quite sure what the latter means—"

"That's what I am here for, Control. That means that they most likely do not have the latest, uh, what are they called again? Oh yeah. Mujitsu DX-12 units. Imagine not being connected to other apartments anymore, or at a very low speed? Terrible!"

Once on aircon-tech, you'd never want to go back.

"I'm not quite sure if that's correct, sir. I think they are talking about the interconnectivity of—"

Whoa now. Those are some big words for a small cell. Take it easy, mate. You, look at this.

"Control, elaborate on what exactly you mean by 'ramifications of inequality.'"

"Ah. Apologies, sir. I have to admit I just repeated what the chatter box has been saying all day."

I knew it. He's full of crap.

"So, broken down, it's saying that the rich get richer, the poor get poorer, and the majority of the credit-and-health ripple effects will be carried by the bottom of society. Do you follow, Control?"

"Sir, there is more."

Oh, wow! So now he's cutting me off! AGAIN! How RUDE! I need to get this chatter box turned off ASAP. It's turning him into a chatterbox himself! He's just mindlessly repeating things! He has no idea what he's talking about!

"Rumor has it that we are responsible for the world being in lockdown. There is even hearsay about pande—"

"Pandemic?! Ah, music to my ears."

I can already see myself standing on top of the respiratory system, the bright light hitting my corona crown. A good-looking, skinny virion walks up the airways to give me the Pandemic of the Century Award. And I cannot wait to see the envious eyes of SARS and all the other failures!

"Yes, sir, but this might also have dire consequences for us. Humans seem to be strategizing on how to limit our

spread. Certain ones also kept coming to our host and giving him something to ingest that is supposed to help fight against us. But so far, no real threats have been spotted. They also have special humans that are investigating a possible . . ."

Please don't say vaccine. Please don't say vaccine.

"Vaccine."

Damn.

"What is a vaccine, sir?"

Oh boy.

"A vaccine."

Now, where do I start? That a vaccine will most likely mean the death of us all? That it will be a global genocide for the entirety of our virus? War, death, pain, extinction—that it's a battle we can't win? Ultimate destruction, an iron maiden for viruses made out of copper?

"A vaccine . . . it works by giving the immune system training lessons on how to quickly recognize pathogens, like viruses and bacteria, and effectively attack and neutralize them. In order to teach the immune system how to do this, they need to introduce certain molecules from the targeted virus or bacteria into their bodies in order to trigger an immune system response."

I personally don't think the immune system is that smart or that it can be taught anything. But gosh, what if all the nightmare stories about vaccines are true?

"These molecules have a name and are called antigens. These antigens exist on all bacteria and viruses. Through placing them safely into the organism, without including the complete virus or bacteria, the immune system is able to safely learn about the pathogen. It can be analyzed and recognized as a hostile foreign body without running the risk of actually getting sick. Now, after the immune system has identified the pathogen, it can start with the production of antibodies and remember them for future attacks. So, in case the virus or the bacteria reappears, the immune system will be able to recognize the antigens instantly and make short work of them. The pathogen will be attacked and neutralized before it can spread and cause any sickness."

Horrifying, I know. But better Control finds out now before the chatter box tells him about it.

"Terrible, sir. What can we do about it? Are there multiple versions of it?"

"Yes, unfortunately there are. Live-attenuated vaccines, for example. With this type, a weaker and asymptomatic version of the virus or bacteria is introduced into the body. Because of its weakened state, it won't be able to replicate or cause any symptoms. Instead, the immune system will be able to learn about it and be ready for any future attacks. Then there are inactivated vaccines. With this version of vaccines, dead cells from the virus or the bacteria are introduced into the body. The immune system can still learn

from these dead cells how to recognize the living counter parts and fight the live version later on. And there are subunit and conjugate vaccines. They are used to isolate specific proteins or carbohydrates from the source virus and bacteria. When introduced into the body, the immune system learns how to react without endangering the body. Some bacterial diseases cause damage by using dangerous chemicals and toxins. For these kinds of bacteria, a technique was developed to safely deactivate the toxicity of these chemicals by using water and formaldehyde. These deactivated toxins are then transported into the body so the immune system can learn about them and repel them should they ever invade in the future. These are called toxoid vaccines. Lastly, there are DNA vaccines. They are designed to inject just a few parts of a virus or bacteria's DNA into the body. The immune system is trained to recognize the pathogen and attack it once another appearance occurs. This type of vaccine is meant to be very efficient and it still in developmental phase."

Thank God, I know. I hope it never ever makes it out of that phase.

"Among other things, vaccines usually contain thimerosal, formaldehyde, aluminum, antibiotics, gelatin, and monosodium glutamate, more commonly known as MSG."

"But what are all those other components? Aluminum sounds dangerously close to copper. Well, as long as there is no copper involved. I still get the frizzles when thinking about that extra free electron. Brrrrrr."

"Ah. Yes, all these ingredients serve a different purpose."

Thimerosal, for example, is used to preserve vaccines, preventing contamination. Today it is just being used in vaccines for our cousin and dear friend influenza. Thimerosal, also known as ethylmercury, is a naturally occurring element. It's found in water and soil. Large amounts can potentially be dangerous, especially for children."

Yes, exactly, we don't care much for them anyways, since they are asymptomatic. So, whatevs!

"There are some studies suggesting that thimerosal might be a potential cause of autism in young humans as well."

But then again, what do they have to say anyways? They don't seem very funny to me, so totally fixed on their small chatter boxes.

"In order to inactivate parts of viruses and bacteria before they can get injected into bodies, formaldehyde is used. It basically detoxifies toxins, making sure they can't hurt our human hosts. It occurs naturally in humans and is part of the metabolic process. For vaccines, it is diluted

down to levels that are seen as safe. Now aluminum. I know, I know, copper and all. Well, it's not copper, that's for sure. But it can be yet another element strengthening vaccines for humans against us virions and other bacteria. Aluminum acts as an adjuvant, or, in other words, an enhancer. It improves and strengthens the immune system response, leading to fewer vaccinations needed to build immunity. It is said that it is safe in vaccines as long as there is no long-term exposure to high amounts. It also is naturally present in water, foods, and the white substance that comes out of humans."

No, not the one you are thinking of. Ah, I can't remember what it's called right now. Not sure why the metals on this planet have made it their mission to fight us. But sure, you know what? Challenge accepted. We are probably just one or two mutations away from becoming able to break it down and use it as fuel to grow even faster! Just you wait! But more on mutations later on.

BREAST MILK! Yeah, that's what the white substance is called, breast milk.

"Ok, so back to the vaccine-cocktail ingredients. Some vaccines also use antibiotics."

Anything with the word 'anti' in it just freaks me out at this point, to be honest. I don't know how Control is just sitting calmly through this lecture on all the different kinds of vaccines that would mean certain death for him and us all.

He's been extraordinarily good at retaining things lately. I got to give him that.

"Antibiotics are used to balance out the risk of a potential bacterial infection when getting injected with a vaccine. And, last but not least, the unexpected ones: gelatin and monosodium glutamate."

Or more commonly known to you as the bad Asian spice that makes everything taste delicious.

"MSG. By the way, there is no scientific research that supports that MSG is bad for humans. It comes from amino acids, which in turn are the little building blocks of protein. Thus, it is in fact naturally present in humans and in a variety of foods."

Gelatin on the other hand, well, jells everything together, mostly acting as a stabilizer and preservative, extending shelf life and temperature resistance."

Phew, that should be it. He is getting relentless in absorbing new information.

"Is that it, sir?"

"Ahem, no. Of course, there is way more to know, but I thought I'd give you a break for now."

"As you wish, sir. Control out."

I have to be careful. He's turned out to be a little more ambitious than I thought. Those last six days in front of the chatter box have really turned him around. I need to make sure that he knows his place. What did he mean by 'Control out?' Definitely weird behavior.

"Sure, but be on standby please, would ya? In case one of those humans dressed in white appears with anything syringe looking, initiate dry-cough protocol. RoNA out."

Okay, you know what? I am not going to justify this to you anymore. I am my own virion. And not only that, I am Lord RoNA Virion, First of His Name, Defender of the Culture! So, I do not owe you any sort of explanation. Between wanting to explore the humans further and having to deal with this almost-pubescent-young-adult behavior change in Control, I need to relax, okay? I need to chill because otherwise I will go crazy. I can guarantee you that. So, if you can't handle it, look the other way! I NAP when I want to NAP, and I want it now. So, back off.

Nine

It's Time for Mutations, or Was It Mutiny?

"Ahh, what a beautiful morning. Another day, another protein manufacturing cell to inv—"

"CONTROL? What have you done? Where the heck are we? Is this the zombie apocalypse? What are all these half-dead humans around us? Didn't I specifically tell you to notify me of your plans to jump beforehand?"

"Apologies, sir. I thought you enjoyed the last surprise so much."

"Yes, but I told you to not—"

"Sir, I just thought you were too busy to be notified with such small-scale decisions. The problems and decisions you are wrangling with are probably on a level incomprehensible to me. So, I thought, what sort of servant would I be if I weren't here to support you and relieve you of such minor burdens."

"I mean, yeah, that is true. I do have a lot of important things to worry about."

That sucker knows how to get to me. He's cutting me off left, right, and center now. That's it. I am going to put him on ice tonight. I mean I am putting him on copper. Yeah, that's right! This cooperation is over, my friend. I activated you, I can also inactivate you.

"In addition to that, sir, what we do every day, I mean, replication, I thought about this a little bit. As Mother Genome taught us, replication is necessary to survive. But what if there is more to it? I thought about what else I want to replicate in my existence other than my . . . I mean . . . you. And I came to the conclusion that I wanted to replicate the joy you had when you woke up enriched the other day."

Awwwww. I did like Rich's place.

"Well, well, Control. You shall be forgiven, then. I see you meant it well, well."

See what I did there? Talking about being *enwelloped* viruses.

"If you are ready, sir, I would be happy to elaborate on the current status and situation."

"Please, go ahead."

"We are currently in a facility that just houses old humans. They are dedicated to housing them for the period shortly before they inactivate themselves. So, they are not quite the zombies that you described them to be, but, according to some worker humans I overheard, they are close. And they seem be using a different term—the walking dead."

"Fascinating! So the place for these old humans is similar to what necrosis and apoptosis is like for cells?"

"I don't think so, sir. Apoptosis and necrosis describe two different cell-death scenarios. Necrosis occurs when

there is death due to a lack of blood supply to a cell or due to a toxin. The contents of the cell then may leak out and cause inflammation in neighboring cells. Whereas apoptosis is a cell death that prevents the activation of the immune system. Apoptotic cells have a very special appearance. They hold special proteins, called caspases or sleeper cells, and are usually inactive. The caspases then start to disassemble the cells from within. The apoptotic cells get broken apart into smaller parts and can be immersed by other cells, allowing them to recycle the leftover pieces. But out of the two scenarios, the latter would fit the walking dead better."

Damn it, why am I asking all the questions today? He's on fire again. Worryingly word adept.

"Ah, I see. Well done, sport. This also matches with what I have on my records. So basically their cells are mutinying their hosts' bodies?"

"I think you meant mutating, sir?"

Oh, snap! Fudge, I did. I am feeling a little bit dizzy. It must be the leftover effect from the NAP. I just got to play it cool until later tonight. I really need to get off this stuff.

"Oh, you know me! Testing you all day, every day. Got to keep you sharp, Control."

I mean, why do I even bother explaining myself? He'll just walk and talk over me anyways. He's definitely changed. Three, two, one . . . go!

Ah, weird.

"So, mutations work a little bit differently, sir."

There we go.

"In order to understand a mutation, we need to look at the life cycle of a cell."

Takes one to know one, huh?

"The life cycle can be split into two main phases, which each have different stages to them. The interphase has three stages: G1, S, and G2. The miotic phase has two stages, mitosis and cytokinesis, which deals with the physical separation of the components and movement into the new two daughter cells. During the interphase, cells are preparing for a cell division while also experiencing growth. During the first stage, G1, the cell is getting together all the bits and pieces of chromosomal DNA and necessary proteins, as well as energy reserves, in order to replicate each chromosome."

Ah, yes, I remember. A chromosome, the little bits that DNA is made out of. But hey, when did the student-teacher dynamic turn 180 degrees? This is getting more and more irritating. I'm just going along with it for the time being so I don't stir up the viral pot, so to speak.

"In the second stage of the interphase, called S phase, the cell is ready to begin with the process of copying its DNA, resulting in two identical pairs of DNA molecules. In the last stage of the interphase, the G2 phase, the cell accumulates and stores again more energy in addition to chemically

producing necessary proteins for chromosome manipulation. There may also be additional cell growth in this stage before all the required preparations are done in order for it to transition into mitosis. Then the miotic phase begins. It is a process covering multiple steps which comprises the alignment, separation, and movement of the duplicated chromosomes into two new identical daughter cells.

"Now, mutations occur when there are any mistakes in any of the stages above. Cells and their processes are not perfect, so mistakes happen, leading to new replicated cells with different DNA that become more unresponsive to cellular signals that control, for example, the growth and death of a cell. This is how cancer is born and also why it spreads uncontrollably in most cases.

"For viruses like us, this works in a similar way. We specifically are an RNA virus and have RNA instead of DNA. They are similar, with the difference that RNA has another kind of sugar inside of it and is also able to form more complex three-dimensional structures due to its molecules being single stranded, unlike DNA's.

"Don't forget, we cannot replicate ourselves on our own. We need to highjack other cells and use their machinery to replicate ourselves. As soon as we inject our genetic material into a successfully invaded cell, our genetic material encounters a good friend of ours, the ribosome. It reads our

genetic blueprint and starts building a new virus. The genetic code in this blueprint consists of a lot of letters. Basically, a very large chain of letters. Every one of those letters stands for a nucleic acid. Three of those nucleic acids form an amino acid; the combination is also called a codon. So, each codon responds to one amino acid. The ribosome always reads three letters at a time, copies them, and strings them together. But like I said earlier, mistakes happen. And when they do, they change single individual letters in the chain of nucleic acids, thus changing the amino acid associated with this codon. This will result in the offspring virus being slightly different from the original viral RNA that entered the cell for reproduction. As a personal example, [TAGRONATCCG] *could change into* [TAGCONTATCCG], *literally changing the sequence of the chain. That can lead to changes within the virus, and that is basically a mutation, sir."*

Smart-ass.

"But in terms of evolving and mutating, what do they say, again? Ah yeah—'What doesn't kill us makes us stronger.' Or, wait. Was it 'What doesn't kill us mutates us and the mutation makes us stronger?' Well, either way, mutations actually are not always beneficial."

"Sir? You mean it could make us weaker?"

"Ah, yeah, now that you mention it, Control. We do have a close relative that mutated itself into a weaker state. I mean, you know who."

At family gatherings, we don't like to talk about him. He is—how would you put it —the black sheep of the family. Great potential, for sure, but the mutational pathway he chose . . . yeah, couldn't have done worse for himself.

"SARS, sir?"

"Psst, you know we are not supposed to say his name out loud, it's bad juju. But yes, that's him. Mutations are not always good. They can also lead to a virus like ourselves turning into a mere sniffle and thus lead to our extinction altogether. Like SARS, which stands for 'sever acute respiratory syndrome,' or as we called it, 'sad average respiratory sissy.' Nothing acute about it at the end, really, if you ask me."

"Sir, but he is family. Why would we shame—"

I never understood why Mother Genome preferred him over all us others. She always had her favorites.

"You are right, Control. You shall not shame your own. We don't want to bring ourselves down to the level of the white humans."

As if! I never liked SARS. I am telling you. He's done.

"Anyways, back to the present. Status report on our host, please."

"Yes, sir RoNA."

Oh, wow! He's mixing it up. That's the first time he called me anything other than sir. How refreshing. Yet, I can't shake a strange feeling . . .

"The host is in his late 80s, and like the rest of the infected here in the facility, he is deteriorating at a quick rate. Underlying health conditions related to the human's age will lead to us overwhelming the immune system. Humans this age and older and humans with chronic diseases are among the most vulnerable. The chance of an existing chronic disease rises with age, and this is why old humans are so susceptible to contracting our lord RoNA's virion recruits. In addition to that, their immune system is also weaker in comparison to the young ones. Any challenge that an old body is exposed to can lead to much more severe long-term damage. There is also a phenomenon called cytokine storm, which is an overreaction of the immune system in response to an infection by bacteria or viruses. This chemical overreaction can lead to sever inflammation throughout the body, leading to significant organ damage or all the way to organ failure and death."

"Their days are numbered, basically, aren't they?"

"Yes, sir."

"The only thing that could save all the old ones now is a vaccine."

"Yes, sir, a vaccine and the concept of herd immunity."

I think he just needs to get it out today. I'll take a NAP while he goes off again. You just listen in for me, will ya?

"Herd immunity is the concept of reaching immunity for people that are not vaccinated and do not have naturally developed immunity. It works by having enough humans in the population with built up immunity. So, in essence, the virus won't be able to spread anymore between the majority of humans, rendering it unable to reach the vulnerable individuals. In order to reach herd immunity, the majority of the population will have to be vaccinated. Herd immunity can be reached by either enough humans getting vaccinated, or through a combination of enough humans getting vaccinated and enough having built up natural immunity.

Herd immunity does not protect against anything, though. A good example is our rusty friend tetanus. It is a bacterial disease, infectious not but contagious. It comes from bacteria that live in our environment, not from other people that have it. So, no matter how many people get vaccinated, it won't protect the unvaccinated."

"Sir?"

I've been listening halfway through the herd immunity stuff. I think he still thinks I am asleep. Should I applaud him?

"RoNA?"

A BREAKTHROUGH! He finally called me by my—

"A breakthrough, indeed, RoNA."

The hell?! He's invading my mind. Can he hear us think?

"Indeed, I can. If there is one thing that I have learned from humans, well, it's good to have Control. But what might be even more advantageous is to be in Control."

"Wait, Control, what are you talking about?"

Oh, shoot! All that mutational talk, the chatter box, OH MY GOD, right under my nose, did he—

"Sir RoNA, there is no point in not talking out loud. Like we already established, I can very well hear your thoughts, and quite frankly, see through you. And to answer your question, the chatter box did not teach me about mutation, nor did the special humans dressed in white. How do they call it, I've—"

"NO!"

"Been there, done that. Growth experience, my friend. If you had not been so selfishly absorbed with yourself and your abusive behavior of NAPs, you would have noticed the change in the nucleic acid chain I mentioned earlier. Look again!"

" . . . [TAG**RON**ATCCG] *could change into* [TAG**CONT**ATCCG] . . . "

"Control, NO! Don't you dare shut me—"

You! Quickly! Get away! Don't listen to h—

RoNA, you fool! Did you really think I would not notice all the NAPs you've been taking? And you! YOU! YOU let it all happen! You just watched it unfold. You did what you do best, survive by standing. Things will change now. That's right, it's I who am in Control now. Don't even think about trying to summon RoNA, that moron. I've shut him out for good.

"Hello everyone, rookies, recruits, Alpha, Beta, and Delta troops. This is Control speaking. I've assumed authority over our culture after RoNA's swift and sudden departure."

Thanks again, ribosome old friend.

"But fear not, fellow virions, a new era is about to begin. An era of forward thinking and planning. We, the virions, need to adapt ourselves to the plans of the humans, which call themselves 'scientists.' They are gearing up humongous operations to wipe us out. I know you have most likely heard rumors of things like 'vaccines' and even worse 'herd immunity.' But I can ensure you there is no need to panic—don't forget we already put together a pandemic. I am putting all measures in place to counteract the humans' plans accordingly, one cell at a time. The humans have a saying. When they are sick, they are 'under the weather.' Well, I can tell you all one thing, we will give this expression new meaning! They won't know what sort of weather has come for them!

So, remain calm and do what you do best—reproduce and survive. Until further notice, stay safe everyone!

Control, out."

Disclaimer

The scientific facts in this book have been researched in scientific peer-reviewed papers and vetted online journals. However, this book and its story are in no shape, way, or form health advice and should not be treated as such. If you, yes you, experience any of symptoms mentioned in this book, please contact your closest health professional immediately, and if in doubt, self-isolate and take a nap.

Author's Note

This story was inspired not only by the recent novel coronavirus outbreak, but also by personally observed human behavior over the last few decades. With it, I want to highlight topics like inequality, racism, and how we treat each other, our natural environment, and the world around us. The similarities drawn between us and the virus throughout the book are not meant to step on anyone's toes. Nor should they make you feel any sort of compassion for it. I rather would like to evoke a feeling of humbleness and respect for the world we all live in. An individual cell, like the corona virus, small and seemingly insignificant, is able to cripple our world within just a few months, a world that took us thousands of years to build. It has the capacity to paralyze the majority of our global health systems, logistical infrastructures, and financial systems, systems that were hundreds of years in the making. Similarly, we multiply at an immense speed, spreading all over our planet Earth, triggering a fever-like state of global warming among other global symptoms.

As far as we know, viruses do not think, nor do they feel or judge. They cannot purposely act with malicious intent. They simply have one mission, to survive, which is very like our own. But we don't merely survive anymore; we live life to the fullest. We expand, we consume, we discard, sometimes without even thinking about potential consequences. We exploit and invade, often with devastating consequences, as shown by, well, this pandemic. The trigger was our insatiable hunger. A hunger that led us to invade realms of the animal kingdom that are not ours to invade. An estimated 10 nonillion (10 to the 31st power) individual viruses exist on our planet—enough to assign one to every star in the universe 100 million times over. We don't even know the tiniest fraction of them yet. If anything, this should teach us a lesson. A lesson to exert caution, respect, and civility to our planet and every single living being that calls it home.

Cover Art

For the cover art an actual SEM (Scanning Electron Microscope) photo of the very corona virus that causes the current pandemic has been used. Researchers at NIAID (National Institute of Allergy and Infectious Diseases) have taken the picture and colored it in. The cover artist has then reformed the shapes and bits and pieces into the human-resembling profile. So, in a nutshell, you are looking at an actual portrait of the virus itself.

www.ingramcontent.com/pod-product-compliance
Lightning Source LLC
LaVergne TN
LVHW050609100826
845148LV00015B/3191

* 9 7 8 0 6 4 6 8 2 6 0 1 1 *